Danny, Bee and the Skunk

written and photographed
by
Mia Coulton

"Look at the cat," Danny said to Bee. "Let's chase the cat up the tree."

"Here we come,"

barked Danny.

Danny and Bee got very close to the cat. The cat did not run away.

Danny stopped and looked at the cat.

"Oh, no!" Danny said.

"That is not a cat. That is a skunk!"

Danny ran away fast.

Off came Bee.

Bee got skunked!

P.U.

Skunk   Out

to   the   rescue.